Victorious Paints the Great Balloon

LES AÉRONAUTES
PAR
VICTORIOUS RATTAN

Victorious
Paints
the
Great Balloon.

By David Francis Birchman • Illustrated by Jonathan Hunt

Bradbury Press • New York

Collier Macmillan Canada • Toronto
Maxwell Macmillan International Publishing Group
New York • Oxford • Singapore • Sydney

Bradbury Press
Macmillan Publishing Company
866 Third Avenue
New York, NY 10022

Collier Macmillan Canada, Inc.
1200 Eglinton Avenue East
Suite 200
Don Mills, Ontario M3C 3N1

First edition
Printed and bound in the United States of America
by Horowitz/Rae
1   2   3   4   5   6   7   8   9   10

The text of this book is set in Scotch.
Book design by Cathy Bobak

Library of Congress Cataloging-in-Publication Data
Birchman, David Francis.
Victorious paints the great balloon / by David Francis Birchman.
p.   cm.
Summary: Victorious, a member of the unlucky Rattan family in rural France, becomes involved in a historic hot air balloon ascension and restores good repute to the Rattans.
ISBN 0-02-710111-8
[1. Hot air balloons—Fiction.   2. Balloon ascensions—Fiction.   3. Montgolfier, Jacques-Etienne, 1745–1799.   4. Montgolfier, Joseph-Michel, 1740–1810.   5. France—Fiction.]   I. Title.
PZ7.B511877Vi   1991
[E]—dc20   90-1746

To Diane and all her animals
—D.F.B.

For my brothers,
Chris, Cris, and Jerry,
who keep finding new ways to make me laugh
—J.H.

Contents

Illustrations

A NOTE FROM THE ARTIST

The paintings for *Victorious Paints the Great Balloon* were done on 140 lb. hot press
watercolor paper. The full-color pictures were painted using transparent watercolors.
The black-and-white halftone illustrations were painted in Payne's gray watercolor
using a full range of values. They were reproduced for the book in black ink. The
Rattan family crest was designed in keeping with traditional heraldic imagery.

Singing Fish
and
Stuffed Dragons

A woeful description of calamities caused by
the absence of fish and the presence of dragons

In the little village of Aix La Zag . . .

It was a time of great change in France. New ideas were popping out like spring buds. Inventive people were trapping lightning in fruit jars, taking air apart and putting it back together again, and flying down country roads in horseless wagons rigged with sails and puffed along by the power of the wind. The modern world was being born; it was a wonder to behold, and it almost took your breath away to talk about it.

In the little village of Aix La Zag, however,

things were as they had always been. The people there didn't want to hear about new ideas, they didn't want to know about the birth of the modern world, and they didn't want to talk about anything but the things they had always talked about. There were only three things that the people of Aix La Zag had ever talked about— singing fish, dragons, and the very bad luck of Victorious Rattan.

Each year during the spring tide, the fish in the Rhône had come to the village of Aix La Zag to sing. Pilgrims and music lovers would flock in from all over Europe to hear the miracle. Merchants hawked books filled with authentic fish music, underwater kazoos, and silver minnow–size good-luck charms. The wives of fishermen boiled fish whose meat was guaranteed to cure sore throats, hiccups, or a bad singing voice. The bakers baked cakes in the shape of fish, the weavers wove flags in the shape of fish, and the cobblers cobbled shoes in the shape of fish. Everyone in the village made a pretty penny, except the fish.

In the morning there would be a drumroll and

4

all the pilgrims and music lovers would wade out into the Rhône and stick their right ears in the water. As they stood there all wet and shivering, delight would gradually spread over their faces; a delight that could only come from hearing the sound of a school of singing fish.

That is how it had always been. The fish would sing, the pilgrims and music lovers would listen, and the villagers would count their pretty pennies. But the world was changing, and people were changing, too. The trouble began with just a few pilgrims and an occasional music lover grumbling that they couldn't hear the fish very well. Each year there was just a bit more grumbling. And a bit more grumbling. Large numbers in the crowd began to complain that all they were getting for their trouble were empty pockets, cold feet, and wet ears. The grumbling continued to grow louder as the crowds got smaller. Eventually the year arrived when only a single pilgrim wandered into the village, and he was carrying a fishing pole.

"It's all the fault of the fish," complained the mayor. "I never did trust the fish."

There would be a drumroll and all the pilgrims and music lovers would wade out into the Rhône.

"Without the crowds coming to hear the singing fish we will all be ruined," whined the baker. "This is simply horrible. This is as horrible as when the dragon swallowed half the village."

It had been several thousand years since the dragon swallowed half the village, but the people of Aix La Zag had never forgotten it. They told and retold the story of the dragon's visit a hundred different ways. According to most versions of the story, the air about the countryside had been thick with sulphur and smoke for many days before the dragon's arrival. The sun was dim and the sky was washed in a milk white haze, as if it were going to snow. Ash began to fall over the village, covering the rooftops and the cobbled streets. The villagers walked about the streets with their noses pointed toward the sky and their scarves about their mouths. They shook the ash from their boots and shuddered. No one knew what was going to happen, but they all knew it was going to be horrible.

And it was horrible! At first the dragon appeared to be no more than a strange dark cloud in the milk white sky, but soon the cloud grew blue and monstrous. The dragon was a thousand feet of fang, fire, and ferocity. In the slit of its eyes there was a glow like burning gold. It briefly hovered over the village with its huge wings beating the air. Then suddenly, like a massive dart, it fell upon the roofs of the houses belching smoke and roaring like—well, like a dragon.

Fortunately it was late in the day, and the dragon was somewhat stuffed after eating a monastery and a small herd of cows, so he ate only half the village and nibbled on the roof of the cathedral where all the villagers were hiding. Nevertheless, it was horrible enough, and the villagers never stopped fretting over it. Most of the roofs in the village were now covered with dragon-proof shingles, and even though it had all happened several thousand years ago, someone was always predicting the dragon's immediate return. Someone was always pointing out how it looked and smelt like dragon weather.

"This is horrible, simply horrible," whined the baker, who tended to repeat himself. "We should

So he ate only half the village and nibbled on the roof of the cathedral.

have let the dragon finish off the village. Better a quick end than lingering poverty."

"It's all the fault of the fish," griped the mayor. "We depended on them and those slippery fish let us down."

"Nobody has luck as bad as this," exclaimed the cobbler. "Nobody except Victorious Rattan."

The Luck
of the
Rattans

A brief history of the decline of the family Rattan
and the particular and peculiar plight of
Victorious Rattan

The moat turned green, the swans turned green.

The family Rattan had for many centuries been the most prosperous family in the village. The splendid Château Rattan, with its forty-two turrets, meandering maze gardens, swan-stocked moats, and forest filled with tropical howler monkeys, had been built with Rattan prosperity and good luck. The Rattans were judges, lawyers, doctors, and occasionally bishops. It was always a Rattan who led the drumroll to wake up the singing fish on the morning of the spring tide.

Lamentably, Victorious's great-grandfather had lost part of the family fortune when he built a factory to produce dragon-proof roof shingles. The shingles sold like hot cakes in the village of Aix La Zag, but like cold mush everywhere else. Victorious's grandfather then sank more of the Rattan fortune into a fleet of trading ships that immediately sank to the bottom of the sea. Victorious's father, Hercules Rattan, tried to make up for these losses by starting a silkworm farm. He became a rather good farmer, but lost even more of the Rattan fortune before discovering that people wanted the silk from the worms and not the worms themselves. The villagers began to talk about the rotten luck of the Rattans and no longer wanted them to lead the drumroll to wake up the singing fish.

What with the shingles and the sinking ships and the silkworm losses, the family simply did not have enough money to keep up the Château Rattan. The turrets began to crumble and topple, the maze gardens became so overgrown that visitors lost their way in them for weeks at a time, the moat turned green, the swans turned green, and the tropical howler monkeys abandoned the forest and lived in the unused rooms of the châ-

16

teau. And it was into the middle of this world going to ruin that Victorious Rattan was born.

Victorious spent his boyhood wandering the château with his sketchbook, drawing pictures of cracks, crumbling walls, and vines dripping through the broken windows. Sometimes he'd stop in one of the dark hallways to copy a dust-covered portrait of an ancient Rattan. His enormous artistic talent bloomed almost before he could talk. Often his parents would find him on his stomach studying the yellowed and torn books in the family library, gazing at pictures of ruined cities and abandoned temples.

By the time Victorious reached his eighteenth birthday, the family Rattan decided he would leave the Château Rattan to earn his way in the world as an artist and architect. Everybody knew Victorious would be a huge success—but he wasn't.

Things went well enough at first. Victorious's talent was so enormous that he became an overnight sensation. People with money and vanity to spare adored his flattering portraits. They didn't even mind that the figures in his paintings always seemed a bit too young and a bit too beautiful. Princes ordered large bronze heroic statues of themselves sitting on round, oversized, muscular horses with their swords raised high and their spurs dangling low. Cities pleaded for his work. He designed fountains heaped and boiling with spouting cupids and tangled sea creatures. He designed cloud-high bell towers and majestic egg-domed cathedrals.

Victorious would have certainly led a life of endless artistic triumph had it not been for a singular oddity about his work: It never lasted. It always fell apart. It was soon destroyed. It toppled over. It quickly crumbled into dust. The smiles on the beautiful faces in all his paintings began to sag almost as soon as the paint dried. The cupids and tangled sea creatures in his fountains would begin spurting rust. His majestic egg-domed cathedrals always cracked open. Bats refused to hang in his bell towers. Princes who ordered statues from him were always overthrown; their bronze figures astride the round, oversized, muscular horses were pulled down, melted, and made into cannonballs.

Why his artwork didn't last baffled poor Victorious. He had not even noticed the problem while he was living in the Château Rattan, where everything was already in a state of decay.

"Perhaps," he thought, "it is simply the rotten Rattan luck."

Whatever the reason, his success as an artist ended and he was soon destitute. He wrote his father announcing that he would be returning to the Château Rattan. His father wrote him back a rather chatty letter telling how the long winter had been hard on the silkworms. It had, in fact, forced him into raising wooly caterpillars, which were much harder to shear than sheep. Toward the end of his letter Hercules Rattan noted that it might be difficult for Victorious to return home at present because the villagers were very upset now that the singing fish were no longer singing. They were, it seemed, quite down on anything or anyone smacking of bad luck.

Stuffing his father's letter in his coat pocket, Victorious did what most Frenchmen do when they can think of nothing else to do. He started on the road to Paris.

Painting
the
Great Balloon

Wherein Victorious paints and panics
and barnyard animals go ballooning

. . . customers were so pleased with his work that they would reward him with . . . a barnyard animal.

It was a time of great change in France. It was a time of *greater* change in Paris. New ideas were popping out like spring buds. Astronomers were discovering how the heavens brewed moonshine. Geologists were discovering that rocks weren't born yesterday. Inventive minds were finding out how to put bouillon into cubes, tuna into tin cans, and everything you ever wanted to know into an enormous book called an encyclopedia. The modern world was being born. It was a wonder to behold, and it almost took your breath away to talk about it. There was one thing that *did* take your breath away to talk about—man was beginning to fly.

As Victorious marched along the road to Paris, he stopped here and there to earn his supper by painting barns and fashioning wonderful-looking weathervanes. Sometimes customers were so pleased with his work that they would reward him with a little money or a barnyard animal. By the time Victorious reached Paris his pockets were heavy with copper and he was accompanied by a duck, a rooster, and a sheep. They followed him down the great boulevards of the city quacking, crowing, and bleating at the wonderful sights all about them.

The boulevards were alive with the traffic of the great city. The idle and the busy mixed into one massive swirling crowd. Housewives haggled with vegetable vendors, hucksters hawked and hoodwinked, and jugglers juggled in front of jammed audiences while pickpockets picked from behind. On every corner people stood about chattering over the news of the day. There were soldiers on horses, women with bright parasols leaning out of carriages, and large splendid coaches loaded with large splendid people.

One such large splendid coach drew up alongside Victorious as he was gawking at the crowd. A gold-knobbed cane thrust itself out of the window and began rapping for the driver to stop. The door of the coach flew open and a large splendid man with gold leggings, a brocaded silk coat, a powder-white periwig, and a pinched nose glared down at Victorious and his little group.

"I, Marquis Buzot Briszot de L'Buzzonne, minister extraordinaire to His Majesty Louis XVI, do hereby appoint these creatures the first aeronauts of all France."

"Baaaaah," baaaaahed the sheep.

"Cauk-a-doooodle doooo," cauk-a-doooodled the rooster.

"Quack," quacked the duck.

"What?" gasped Victorious.

"Balloons," replied the Marquis Buzot Briszot de L'Buzzonne. "These beasties are going to ascend into the heavens in a great balloon."

"I . . . do hereby appoint these creatures the first aeronauts of all France."

Before Victorious could collect his wits, the little group was all collected inside the coach and whisked away to the court of Versailles.

The balloon, an egg-shaped bag seventy feet long, was spread out on a large platform that had been erected in the middle of an open courtyard. Bales of straw, which would be burned later to inflate the balloon, were hidden under the platform. Joseph-Michel and Jacques-Étienne Montgolfier, the two brothers who invented the great balloon, were busily directing the preparations for its flight.

The Marquis L'Buzzonne's lips closed tighter and his nose grew sharper as he descended from the coach and briskly strode toward the platform. He spent a long moment shaking his head as he stared at the limp balloon. "No, no, no, no, no," he said disdainfully. "This balloon is just paper and canvas. It is ugly. Do you expect His Majesty Louis XVI to watch the voyage of a common paper bag? It must be painted."

"Paint the balloon?" exclaimed Joseph-Michel Montgolfier. "But we have no time to paint the balloon."

"The balloon will be painted by tomorrow morning," snapped the Marquis L'Buzzone. "We will have no common paper bag." He then quickly pointed to the animals sitting beside Victorious in the coach. "These by the way are your aeronauts."

"Baaaaah," baaaaahed the sheep.

"Cauk-a-doooodle doooo," cauk-a-doooodled the rooster.

"Quack," quacked the duck.

"Excuse me," said Victorious as he climbed down from the coach with the duck under one arm and the rooster under the other. "I am an artist, and I would be quite honored to paint your balloon."

. . .

Great quantities of paint had to be purchased and mixed before the work could begin. This task was not completed until evening. Finally, Victorious began to brush the entire surface of the balloon with a deep azure blue. The blue, of course, was for the sky.

While the blue surface of the balloon was drying, Victorious had torches placed all about so he could work through the night. He then began again by painting the signs of the zodiac in a rich gold at the top of the balloon. This, of course, was for the stars in the heavens. Around the middle of the balloon he painted three enormous suns, each about twenty feet high, each with the face of His Majesty. Just above the suns he placed a broad band of color which resembled a theater curtain. Sections of this band were held up by the jowls of lions. Then in a flourish he festooned the entire balloon with exotic filigree and a thousand flying birds.

"I do hope I haven't forgotten anything," thought Victorious as he gazed at the balloon. "Perhaps I ought to add a dozen winged putti fluttering about the suns or a storm of howling comets streaking across the middle. . . ."

He then heard the sound of birds announcing the coming of day. "Well, no matter. At least it is no longer a common paper bag." Victorious climbed down from the platform, washed himself off, and wandered off to sleep.

Sleepy or not, the artist woke with a start later that morning from a most unhappy dream. In his dream he saw the great balloon, sheep, rooster, and duck, come tumbling out of the sky while a crowd of spectators let out a deafening wail: "It's

"I do hope I haven't forgotten anything," thought Victorious.

the rotten luck of the Rattans. It's that rotten Rattan luck." The great balloon then hit the ground and shattered in a hundred shards like an immense Christmas tree ornament, and the crowd let out an even louder wail: "Oh, why did we ever let Victorious paint the great balloon? *Why did we ever let Victorious paint the great balloon?*"

Victorious hurled himself out of bed, slapped on his shoes, and ran back to the courtyard. By this time all the avenues, the windows, and even the attics leading to the courtyard were filled with spectators. All the citizens of Paris had come to see this new idea pop out and up. With all of Paris at Versailles, it was impossible to see the great balloon, which now had a wicker basket attached to it filled with the three aeronauts.

"Halt," shouted one of his Majesty's soldiers as Victorious rushed up to the platform. "No one is allowed to go near the great balloon."

"But they mustn't send it up."

"Why?" asked the soldier. "All of Paris is here and they are expecting to see something sent up."

31

"Because I painted it," replied Victorious.

"Yes, I see," said the soldier, scratching his head. "And a very fine job you did. I've inspected it myself. A bit too spare for my taste, though. Needs a dozen winged putti fluttering about the suns and a storm of howling comets streaking across the middle."

"Please let me through!" pleaded Victorious.

"Sorry," said the guard. "No one is to go near the great balloon. I've got my orders."

• • •

At that moment, in the main balcony of the court-yard, Their Majesties appeared along with other members of the royal court. The balcony bloomed with costumes of silk and velvet. The ladies wore towering hairdos, some shaped like huge wedding cakes, temples, or battleships. Their faces were painted and powdered, and patched with *mouches* (flies) made of black silk cut in the shape of hearts, teardrops, moons, comets, or stars. Jewels of every precious sort dripped from their necks. Their beauty was awe inspiring; only the gentlemen were prettier.

His Majesty gave a nod, a cannon boomed, and the straw was lit under the platform. The balloon began to inflate almost at once with smoke and hot air. Its folds and pleats spread apart with great speed. The crowd gasped. His Majesty poked Her Majesty on the shoulder and nodded with approval.

The sight of the full balloon was glorious. It rose majestically into the air, pulling the wicker basket and the little group of aeronauts behind it. All of Paris cheered . . . all but Victorious, who moaned and hid his eyes.

Suddenly a gold-knobbed cane rapped on the side of the coach and then rapped Victorious over the top of his head. "Step in, step in, quickly, quickly. We must race the balloon to its landing spot!" exclaimed the Marquis L'Buzzonne. Victorious stumbled into the coach, sat down, and again put his hand over his eyes. "Come, come, painter, it's not all that terrible. I believe Their Majesties rather liked your painting. A bit too spare for my taste, though. Needed a dozen winged putti fluttering about the suns and a storm

It rose majestically in the air, pulling the wicker basket and the little group of aeronauts behind it.

of howling comets streaking across the middle. Nevertheless, it was all quite adequate. Nothing to get upset over."

. . .

The great balloon came down a few miles south of Versailles in the branches of an oak tree. The wicker basket containing the aeronauts gently swayed to the ground. Soon after, a large group of soldiers on horseback followed by several dozen coaches arrived from Versailles.

The Marquis adjusted his periwig, straightened his back, and slowly stepped down from his coach. He kissed the sheep, the rooster, and the duck on both cheeks and hung ribbons about their necks. "This is a great day for all of France," he declared to the people gathered around the great balloon.

"Baaaaah," baaaaahed the sheep.

"Cauk-a-doooodle doooo," cauk-a-dooodled the rooster.

"Quack," quacked the duck.

"Thank goodness," said Victorious.

The Dragon Returns

How Victorious regains the good name of the family
Rattan, disrupting some pigs in the process

The Marquis L'Buzzonne . . . appointed Victorious official guardian of the three aeronauts.

The successful flight of the great balloon brought the Montgolfier brothers fame, fortune, and a full page in the encyclopedia. The sheep, rooster, and duck received permanent amnesty from the kitchen skillet (heroes are seldom, if ever, eaten), and Victorious was given— Well, Victorious was given the great balloon by the Montgolfier brothers, who immediately began devising plans for an even greater balloon. The Marquis L'Buzzonne, who had soon grown weary of being followed by baaaaahs, cauk-a-doooodle doooos, quacks, and the clanging of medals, appointed Victorious official guardian of the three aeronauts.

The next day Victorious had the balloon and the beasts loaded into an ox cart. He had resolved to return to the Château Rattan, make a successful flight over the village of Aix La Zag, and restore his good name and the good fortune of the family Rattan.

When he arrived at the Château Rattan, Victorious knew exactly what to do. With a little help from the family servants he built a proper platform and gathered straw for the bonfire. He also touched up the surface of the balloon with his paintbrush (adding a dozen putti and a storm of howling comets) and polished the medals of the three aeronauts.

On the morning of the flight a strong, cold breeze came blowing down the length of the river Rhône. A little party from the Château Rattan stood with their backs against the wind, wishing for the straw to be lighted so they could warm their hands against the fire. (Only Hercules

Rattan, who had his pockets full of wooly caterpillars, had warm hands.) The balloon whipped and snapped itself against the platform while the three aeronauts huddled low in the wicker basket to avoid the wind.

When all was set, Victorious gave the signal for the lighting of the straw. A flame instantly burst out which rapidly filled the balloon with smoke and hot air.

Suddenly, just as the bag reached maximum inflation, a gust of wind struck it full in the flank, ripping a foot-long tear along the top of the balloon. A little volcano of smoke began to puff out of the tear.

Victorious decided at once to stop the flight, and he yelled out to those feeding the flames with straw to extinguish the fire. Unfortunately, his voice was muffled in the gusting wind and the servants holding the tether ropes thought they heard the command to release the balloon.

"Stars and garters!" yelled Victorious. "Don't let the balloon get away." He at once lunged for and grabbed onto the wicker basket which was by this time several feet off of the ground. It tipped sideways and the three aeronauts were nearly dumped out before Victorious managed to pull himself in.

The balloon, still full of hot air and smoke, wobbled up into the sky, just missing a line of trees. Those on the ground, who had not known at all what to expect, smiled and waved. "Bring me back a cup of sunshine or a couple of whiskers off the face of the man in the moon," shouted up Hercules Rattan.

Victorious covered his eyes. In a matter of minutes the tear in the balloon had doubled in size and the plume of smoke had grown larger. The balloon then began to make a large hissing sound and a slow descent.

• • •

In the village of Aix La Zag a crowd had gathered in the main square with the idea of marching down to the river to throw rocks at the fish. The mayor had just started into his speech about why only fools trust slippery singers when the dragon suddenly appeared over the roof of the cathedral.

The dragon was monstrous; it twitched, jerked, and made unpredictable leaps and bounds as its bright, grotesque body snaked and hissed across the sky. It spewed a river of smoke, and in its huge talons it held a sheep, a rooster, a duck, and Victorious Rattan.

The townspeople were stricken with terror, and they watched dumbfounded as the dragon dropped to the ground just short of the cathedral into a local pigsty.

"The dragon has snatched Victorious," the mayor finally stammered.

"It's his own fault and his own bad luck," cried the baker.

"Well, it probably is," replied the mayor. "Nevertheless, we still can't allow dragons to fly about snatching up people willy-nilly. We'd all better get our pitchforks."

The townspeople gathered up their pitchforks and their wits and approached the pigsty. The dragon's body could be seen at some distance slowly breathing and twitching. Suddenly, Victorious's head popped up right out of the middle of

"The dragon has snatched Victorious," the mayor finally stammered.

its body. "Goodness gracious, slop and swill, are we all here and unbroken?" asked Victorious, slightly dazed and covered in muck.

"Baaaaah," baaaaahed the sheep.

"Cauk-a-doooodle doooo," cauk-a-doooodled the rooster.

"Quack," quacked the duck.

"Oink," oinked a very puzzled pig.

The townspeople stared at Victorious and then at each other. They began to excitedly whisper and jabber. The jabbering quickly grew into a joyous shout. "Victorious has slayed the dragon! Long live Victorious! Too bad for the dragon!"

Victorious and the three barnyard aeronauts were pulled up out of the pigsty and hoisted on the back of the crowd, which marched about the town square shouting and cheering.

"Let's hang the dragon from a pole in the middle of the town," declared the mayor. "People will come from far and wide to see it."

"We can bake cakes in the shape of dragons," said the bakers.

No other village could boast of a hero who had slain a great balloon.

"And weave flags in the shape of dragons," said the weavers.

"And cobble shoes in the shape of dragons," said the cobblers.

"Yes, we will all make a pretty penny," shouted the whole town.

. . .

And so the tattered shreds of what had once been the great balloon were hung up on a pole in the middle of the village of Aix La Zag. Nobody seemed very eager to hear Victorious talk about Paris, or balloons, or new ideas popping out, so he returned to the château with the sheep and the rooster and the duck and the happiness that at least the good name of the family Rattan was finally restored. He spent the rest of his days trying to rebuild the château, and although it sometimes appeared that parts of the château tumbled away faster than he could build, he never really seemed to mind.

Eventually the truth about dragons and balloons came out, but it came out better than you might suppose. When the villagers of Aix La Zag discovered that Victorious had slain a great balloon instead of a dragon, they were doubly proud. Heroes, after all, had been slaying dragons for as long as dragons had been nibbling cathedral roofs. No other village could boast of a hero who had slain a great balloon. So the villagers began to bake, weave, and cobble all sorts of trinkets in the shape of balloons, and visitors flocked in from all over France. Everyone made a pretty penny and almost no one grumbled.

The End

Victorious Paints the Great Balloon is, of course, a work of fiction, but certain facts and events from the early days of ballooning were used in this story.

The wonderful idea for a great balloon first came to Joseph-Michel Montgolfier one day in 1782 while he was sitting by a fire staring at rising curls of smoke. It occurred to him that smoke, a mixture of hot air and particles of carbon, rises because it is lighter (less dense) than the cooler air surrounding it. The next day, to the amazement of his landlady, he sent a small box shooting to the ceiling by filling it with smoke.

The first actual balloon flight took place half a year later in Annonay, France. The Montgolfier brothers owned a paper factory. (It is reported that an early Montgolfier learned the secret of papermaking while being held captive in the city of Damascus during the time of the Crusades.) A large balloon constructed at the Montgolfiers' paper mill was filled with smoke from burning faggots of straw and released into the air. It rose to a height of 7,200 feet.

Joseph-Michel and Jacques-Étienne Montgolfier were also the first to send living creatures into space during the launch of their second great balloon. These creatures were—you guessed it—a sheep, a rooster, and a duck. The second Montgolfier balloon, constructed in Paris in the fall of 1783, resembled "a sort of blue tent with awnings and superb gold [painted] ornaments." (The workers at the Reveillon works in Paris, rather than Victorious,

50

did the painting.) Although this balloon was handsome, it was doomed. When the Montgolfier brothers attempted to launch it, a tremendous rainstorm suddenly moved in. The paper covering the drenched balloon came unglued and fell off in strips.

Fortunately the French king, Louis XVI, who had wasted an entire afternoon watching this disaster, agreed to attend another trial launch. He, however, gave the Montgolfier brothers only seven days to construct another balloon, and he demanded that it be hauled out to his palace at Versailles. Scrambling madly, the Montgolfier brothers and their workers constructed a third great balloon in only five days. This time the launch went off without a hitch, and the large wicker basket containing the animals gently touched down several miles from Versailles.

Even today many people look up with wonder and wave at a great balloon passing overhead. But, imagine what these great balloons looked like to people who lived over two hundred years ago. When a great balloon (this one launched by Alexander Charles and the Roberts brothers) unexpectedly landed in the village of Gonesse, France, the villagers were terror stricken. People came running from everywhere—pitchforks and guns in hand. Finally, one of the villagers plucked up enough courage to fire a round of buckshot into the balloon. A sudden hiss of leaking gas sent everyone flat on their noses. The government of France was so upset over the incident in Gonesse that it had an announcement posted all about the country informing the populace that "Anyone who shall perceive such Globes in the sky, presenting the appearance of a darkened Moon, must therefore be advised that, far from being a terrifying Phenomena, this is nothing but a Machine, made in every case of Taffeta or of light Cloth covered with paper. . . ."

D.F.B.

David Francis Birchman says, "Victorious Rattan and the village of Aix La Zag come from my days as a student in the south of France. I spent happy afternoons napping in a crumbling old windmill where the French writer Alphonse Daudet was said to have dreamed up many of his stories. Most accounts of the early balloon flights of the Montgolfier brothers give only passing reference to a duck, a rooster, and a sheep—the world's first aeronauts. I set out in this story to give credit where credit is due."

Jonathan Hunt searched the countryside around his home for appropriate models for the world's first aeronauts, finally finding a duck, rooster, and sheep at a country fair. "Bravery," the artist says, "was the special quality I was looking for."

Jonathan Hunt is the author and illustrator of *Illuminations*, about which *Perspectives* said, "*Illuminations* takes its place in the alphabet book hall of fame," and the illustrator of *The Mapmaker's Daughter* by M. C. Helldorfer. *Publishers Weekly* called those illustrations "intricate . . . exotic."

j

Birchman
  Victorious paints the
great balloon.

89691
(13.95)